For Joyce Emmie Roberts,
with love
C.C.

For Francesca Garton
who always can . . .
A.T.

First edition for the United States, Canada and
the Philippines published 1988 by Barron's Educational Series, Inc.

First published 1988 by Piccadilly Press Ltd., London, England

Text copyright © Anne Tyrrell, 1988
Illustrations copyright © Caroline Castle, 1988

All inquiries should be addressed to:
Barron's Educational Series, Inc.
250 Wireless Boulevard
Hauppauge, New York 11788

Library of Congress Catalog Card No. 87-35069

International Standard Book No. 0-8120-5939-5

Library of Congress Cataloging-in-Publication Data
Tyrrell, Anne
    Mary Ann always can.
Summary: A little girl discovers that there are some things that
she can do better than her older sister.
    (1. Sisters--Fiction   2. Stories in rhyme)   I. Castle,
Caroline, ill.   II. Title.
PZ8.3.T857Mar 1988   [E]   87-35069
ISBN 0-8120-5939-5

Printed in Portugal
890 987654321

Mary Ann Always Can

Anne Tyrrell
Illustrated by Caroline Castle

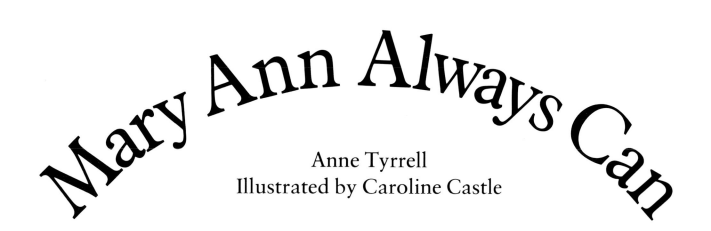

BARRON'S
New York · Toronto

Susan has a sister, her name is Mary Ann,
There are lots of things that Sue can't do,
But Mary always can.

"I can't lace my shoe," says Sue,
"A bow is hard to tie."
"Of course you can," says Mary Ann,
"It's easy if you try."

Because it is so warm today,
Mother says, "Let's swim."
But Susie says, "You know I can't,
I'd better not go in."

And Daddy says, "Of course you can,
Why don't you copy Mary Ann?"
Susie says, "I'd rather get
Just my toes and ankles wet.
I hate it when the water goes
In my ears and up my nose."

All escalators Susie fears,
She simply hates those moving stairs.
"I can't get off in time," says Sue,
"At the end what do I do?"

Mother says, "Of course you can,
Just do the same as Mary Ann."

Uncle Bob who came to stay,
Gave them skipping ropes today.

Susie cannot skip at all,
Each time she tries she has a fall.
"Just copy me," says Mary Ann,
"Then you'll find you easily can."

Mother thinks that ballet would
Do both her girls a lot of good.
Look, everyone is dancing here
But Susie won't join in I fear.

Mary Ann says, "Susie, try.
It is so silly to be shy."

Mother's shown them how to knit,
And Mary Ann's done quite a bit,
Half in purl and half in plain.
Poor Sue has dropped her stitch again.
Mother says, "Just hold it tight
Like Mary Ann – she's got it right."

Then Daddy says, "Please go and see
What time it is, and then tell me.
Which hand is which? How should they go?"
Susie really doesn't know.

"Well I can tell," says Mary Ann.
"I know," sighs Sue, "you always can."

Mary Ann had such a fright,
When lying in her bath last night.

Sitting on the soap beside her
Was a most enormous spider.

Mother came, but they could tell
That she was very scared as well.
"I can't touch that," shrieked Mary Ann,
But Susie said, "Keep calm, I can."
She didn't have a single doubt,
But simply pulled the spider out.

"She is so brave," said Mary Ann,
"I can't do that, but Susie can."

As they walked to school next day,
A barking dog stood in the way.
"He's going to bite," screamed Mary Ann,
She dropped her books and turned and ran.

"He's only talking," Susie said,
And calmly stroked his furry head.
And really Susie was quite right,
He wasn't fierce, but most polite.

Daddy says, "Well I must say,
Sue gets braver every day."
He held her high above his head,
"You're such a clever girl," he said.

From that day onward Susie knew,
There was lots that she could do.
She made a scarf three whole yards long,
And not a single stitch went wrong.
"I've chosen stripes of green and red.
That should suit Daddy," Susie said.

Sue has learned to skip at last,
And now can skip extremely fast.
Forward, backward – sideways too,
WHATEVER NEXT WILL SUSIE DO!

Best of all, she's learned to swim,
And really does enjoy going in.
From the side she makes a dash,
And jumps in with a huge great SPLASH!

It really is so very strange,
There's been a most amazing change,
For Susie now just loves a chance
To show how she can sing and dance.

"No one of four," said Mary Ann,
"Can do as well as Susie can."
She says this rather extra loud,
For Mary Ann just feels so proud.